IKSHIT GAUTAMI

Worthy For a God

Volume 1 : The Beginning

Copyright © 2025 by Ikshit Gautami

All rights reserved. No part of this publication may be reproduced, stored or transmitted in any form or by any means, electronic, mechanical, photocopying, recording, scanning, or otherwise without written permission from the publisher. It is illegal to copy this book, post it to a website, or distribute it by any other means without permission.

This novel is entirely a work of fiction. The names, characters and incidents portrayed in it are the work of the author's imagination. Any resemblance to actual persons, living or dead, events or localities is entirely coincidental.

Ikshit Gautami asserts the moral right to be identified as the author of this work.

Ikshit Gautami has no responsibility for the persistence or accuracy of URLs for external or third-party Internet Websites referred to in this publication and does not guarantee that any content on such Websites is, or will remain, accurate or appropriate.

Designations used by companies to distinguish their products are often claimed as trademarks. All brand names and product names used in this book and on its cover are trade names, service marks, trademarks and registered trademarks of their respective owners. The publishers and the book are not associated with any product or vendor mentioned in this book. None of the companies referenced within the book have endorsed the book.

First edition

This book was professionally typeset on Reedsy.
Find out more at reedsy.com

DECLARATION

I, Ikshit Gautami, declare that this book, Worthy for a God, is my original work. All characters, events, and settings in this book are a work of fiction. Any resemblance to real people, places, or events is purely coincidental.

I confirm that this book has not been published previously in any format and that I hold full rights to its content.

DECLARATION

Contents

Introduction

Ishan Rathore, a young warrior from a legendary bloodline, trains to become strong enough to fight the Asuras—dark beings that threaten humanity. Raised under the guidance of his grandfather, Ravi Rathore, and trained by Sahil Saxena, Ishan discovers his rare ability: the Infinity Eyes, a forbidden power that allows him to trap, destroy, or absorb souls. As he prepares for the Warrior Exam, a grand tournament where warriors from around the world compete, he faces intense training, harsh trials, and growing rivalries.

The Warrior Exam begins, bringing elite fighters to the village, but in the middle of the competition, Dev's left hand man launches a devastating attack. Using an ancient scroll, he summons a Jungle Biome, transforming half the village into a monstrous battlefield filled with millions of Asuras. Forced into an uneasy alliance, Ishan and Ajay Chakravedi, a rival warrior from another country, stand together against the rising chaos. The battle against the Asuras is left unresolved, setting the stage for an even greater war in the next volume.

This volume is a tale of self-discovery, power, and war, leading Ishan toward his ultimate destiny.

Main Characters

Protagonists & Allies:

1. protagonist, a warrior with the power of Infinity Eyes.
2. Rudra Rathore – Ishan's older brother.
3. Rohan Rathore – Ishan's uncle.
4. Karishma Verma – Ishan's aunt.
5. Ravi Rathore – Ishan's grandfather and mentor.
6. Rahul Rathore – Ishan's deceased father.
7. Vijay Rathore – The legendary ancestor of the Rathore Clan.
8. Sahil Saxena – Ishan's teacher who helps train him for the Warrior Exam.
9. Ajay Chakravedi – A skilled warrior from another country, fights alongside Ishan.

Elder Guardians (Leaders of Anti-Asura Community)

1. Surya Dev – First Guardian, strategist of the Anti-Asura forces.
2. Vedika Rai – Second Guardian, master of illusion magic.
3. Yashwant Sen – Third Guardian, experienced warrior.
4. Bhairav Singh – Fourth Guardian, brute-force specialist.
5. Rameshwar Nath – Fifth Guardian, responsible for security.
6. Ravi Rathore – Sixth Guardian (also Ishan's grandfather).

7. Kaushal Thakur – Seventh Guardian, enforcer of discipline.

Antagonists (Enemies):

1. Dev – The main villain, a powerful warrior leading the enemy forces.
2. Dev's Left-Hand Man – Mysterious right-hand of Dev, responsible for summoning the Jungle Biome.

Chapter 1: A New Beginning Born in Blood

A dim fluorescent light flickered in the cold, sterile hallway of the hospital. The air was thick with the scent of antiseptic, yet it couldn't mask the tension that hung in the atmosphere. A man paced anxiously in front of the

operation theater, his fists clenched, his heart pounding.

Five agonizing minutes passed. Then, the door of the OT creaked open. A weary-looking doctor stepped out, his face pale and shadowed with exhaustion.

"Doctor! How is my brother's wife?" the man, Rohan, asked, his voice trembling.

The doctor sighed, removing his mask. "She gave birth to two healthy baby boys... but she didn't survive the operation. I'm so sorry."

Rohan's world collapsed in that moment. His vision blurred as he stumbled back. No. This wasn't supposed to happen. He had promised his brother—he had vowed to protect her. And now...

A gentle hand touched his shoulder. Karishma, his wife, was sitting nearby, her eyes filled with sorrow yet steady with resolve.

"Don't cry, Rohan," she said softly. "This is life. If someone comes into this world, they must leave one day. Instead of grieving, let's focus on the new journey ahead— with the babies."

"But Karishma... I made a promise," Rohan choked, his voice breaking. "I failed. I was so stupid to think I could protect her."

Karishma wiped a tear from his face. "You didn't fail, Rohan. Now, it's your duty to protect these children. Let's raise them with love and give them the life they deserve."

Rohan inhaled sharply, trying to steady himself. "You're right. We have to move forward... But what should we name them?"

Before Karishma could respond, an aged yet commanding voice echoed through the hallway.

"Wait a moment."

Rohan turned swiftly. An old man stood at the entrance, his presence carrying an aura of wisdom and authority.

"Dad?" Rohan whispered in shock. "How did you—?"

"I know everything, Rohan," the old man interrupted. "I came here for a very short time. There's something important I must do." He stepped closer, placing a firm hand on Rohan's shoulder. "The names of your nephews will be Rudra and Ishan—after Lord Shiva himself. The elder one, Rudra. The younger, Ishan."

Rohan blinked. "Rudra... is only one minute older than
    Ishan."

The old man nodded. "That one minute will change
    everything." Then, just as mysteriously as he had appeared, he whispered, "Sayonara." His body faded into thin air, dissolving like dust in the wind.

And so, the new story began.

Five Years Later...

Laughter echoed through the garden as Rudra and Ishan, now five years old, chased each other through the wet grass. The evening sky darkened as storm clouds rolled in.

The first raindrops splattered against the earth, and within moments, heavy rain poured down.

Unfazed by the weather, the boys continued playing near an old underground bunker hidden beneath the overgrown bushes. No one in the neighborhood spoke about the

bunker. It was as if it didn't exist.

Lightning cracked through the sky. BOOM!

A sudden flash of light struck the ground nearby, sending a shock wave through the air. The impact loosened a rusty metal pillar standing in the garden. It tilted dangerously— straight toward Ishan.

Time slowed.

"ISHAN!" Rudra shouted, his instincts kicking in. He lunged forward, shoving his younger brother out of the way.

The pillar came crashing down.

CRACK!

Rudra gasped as the weight slammed into him, crushing his small body. The force of the impact shattered the door to the underground bunker, and before anyone could

react—Rudra's lifeless body fell inside.

Ishan screamed. "RUUDRAAAAAA!!!" His voice tore
    through the night, drowning in the sound of the storm.

Somewhere in the darkness, a whisper lingered.

"Sometimes... a story truly begins after death."

The Descent into Darkness

Ishan collapsed to his knees, sobbing uncontrollably. His aunt and uncle arrived moments later, but instead of comforting him, they began blaming each other for Rudra's death.

"THIS IS YOUR FAULT!" his aunt yelled.

"Mine? He was YOUR responsibility!" his uncle shot back.

Their words stung more than the rain slashing against
   Ishan's face. They don't even care...

Then, he heard something that shattered his heart.

"I don't support Ishan," his aunt muttered coldly. "He's not even my blood. He's just the son of my husband's brother."

Ishan felt his world crumble. Tears streamed down his face. They never saw me as family...

That night, he made a decision. He would leave. He didn't belong here anymore.

But deep beneath the earth, inside the forgotten bunker, something unnatural was happening.

A portal cracked open in the darkness.

A shadowed figure emerged, its glowing eyes fixated on the lifeless body of Rudra. From its hand, a spectral rope slithered out, wrapping around Rudra's spirit—pulling him back from the brink of the afterlife.

"Rudra..." the entity spoke, its voice a chilling whisper.
  "Do you want to live again?"

Rudra's spirit trembled. He looked at his own lifeless body, then up at the figure. "I... I wish I could live longer. I don't want to die yet."

A twisted grin spread across the figure's face. "Then I have an offer for you. Serve me, and I will return you to the world of the living. But... you will no longer be human.

You will be reborn... as an Asura. You must kill humans.
  Hahaha!"

Rudra hesitated. But the desire to live burned inside him.
  "I accept."

The figure stepped forward, drawing a complex ritual circle on the ground. Candles around the room flickered to life on their own. A dark scroll was unfurled, revealing demonic scripture.

A deep hum vibrated through the air as he began chanting an incantation. The walls of the bunker trembled. A torrent of black energy surged around Rudra's body, fusing with his very soul.

A violent explosion erupted.

The Awakening

Above ground , Ishan had just climbed to the rooftop of a neighboring house when a blast of dark energy tore through his home, obliterating it in an instant. The shock wave sent him flying through the air—only to be caught mid-fall by a mysterious figure.

Dazed, Ishan looked up. His home was gone. And standing amid the destruction was Rudra. But he was different. His eyes glowed an unnatural crimson, his body pulsing with raw power.

Ishan's breath caught in his throat. "Rudra...?"

The mysterious figure beside Rudra smirked. "Your brother is no longer yours, boy."

"No... No!" Ishan screamed in agony. "You bastard! Don't take my brother away from me!"

But it was too late.

A portal opened, and the entity pulled Rudra into the darkness. The last thing Ishan saw was Rudra's expression—cold, empty, and no longer human.

Then, he was gone.

Ishan fell to his knees, fists clenched, screaming his brother's name into the void.

The nightmare had only begun.

Then the Ninja take Ishan with him

The dimly lit room smelled of blood and sweat. The air was thick with the metallic scent of iron, and faint echoes of distant screams hinted at the room's dark purpose. The walls were made of stone, damp and cracked, lined with chains and ancient tools of torment. A torture room.

In the center, a boy sat on the cold floor, trembling. His clothes were torn, his body covered in dirt, and his wide, fearful eyes darted around the room. Ishan.

Across from him, a man clad in black robes and a mask sat on a wooden stool, sharpening a kunai. His voice was calm, almost casual.

"Hey, kid," the ninja said, his voice echoing slightly in the eerie silence. "What's your name?"

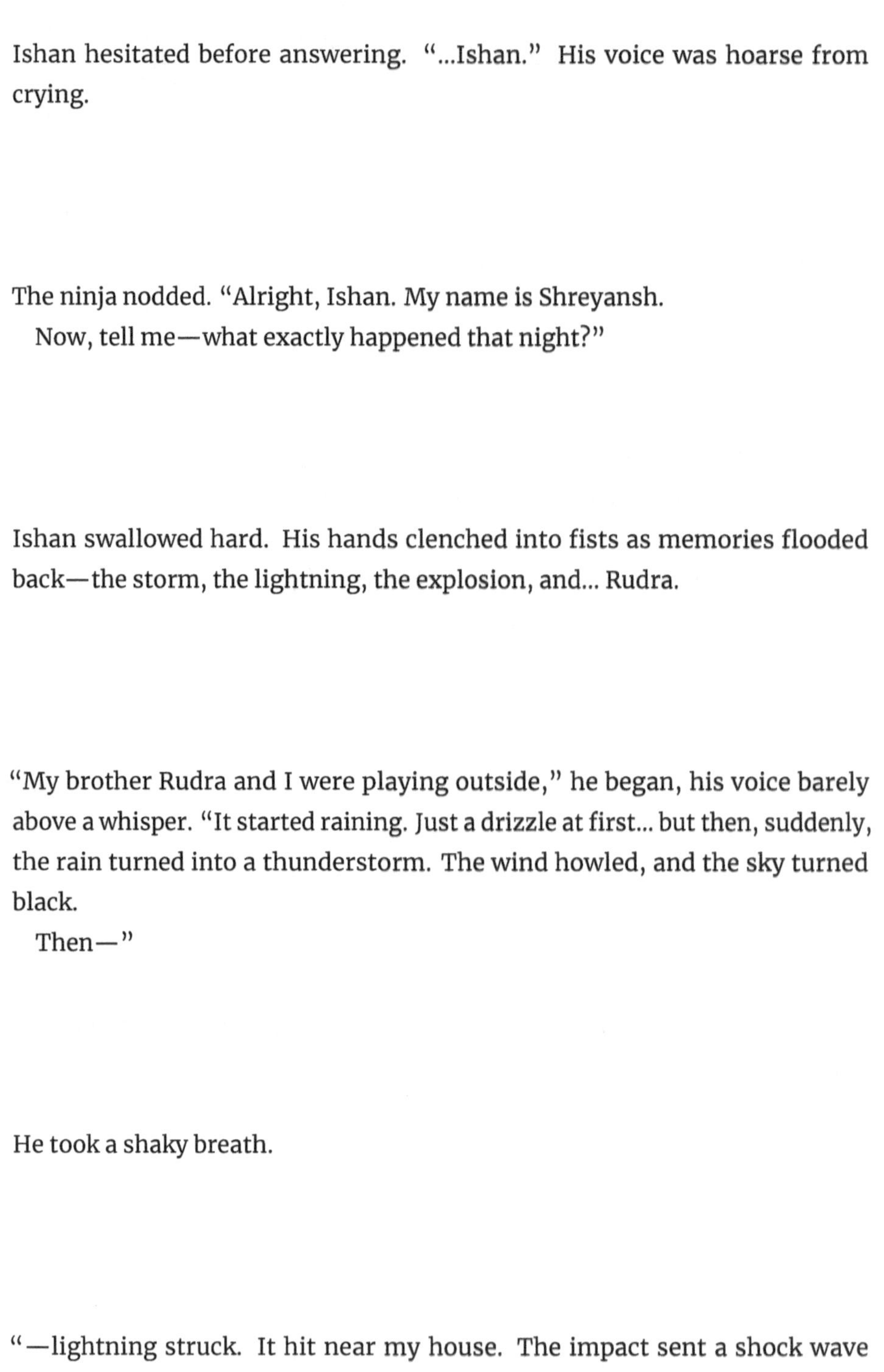

Ishan hesitated before answering. "...Ishan." His voice was hoarse from crying.

The ninja nodded. "Alright, Ishan. My name is Shreyansh.
   Now, tell me—what exactly happened that night?"

Ishan swallowed hard. His hands clenched into fists as memories flooded back—the storm, the lightning, the explosion, and... Rudra.

"My brother Rudra and I were playing outside," he began, his voice barely above a whisper. "It started raining. Just a drizzle at first... but then, suddenly, the rain turned into a thunderstorm. The wind howled, and the sky turned black.
   Then—"

He took a shaky breath.

"—lightning struck. It hit near my house. The impact sent a shock wave through the air. The pole beside me started falling—I didn't even see it coming. But Rudra... he pushed me out of the way."

Ishan's voice cracked. "He saved me... but the pole fell on him instead. It crushed him... and the impact broke the basement door. Rudra... he fell inside."

Silence filled the room. Even Shreyansh, who had heard countless tragic stories, sat still, listening intently.

"I ran," Ishan continued. "I didn't know what else to do. I jumped across rooftops, trying to escape, but then..." He gritted his teeth. "Then... my house exploded."

His breath came faster, his heart pounding. "It wasn't just the house. The entire ground beneath it—gone. Everything was wiped out... down to the basement."

Shreyansh exchanged a glance with another ninja standing in the shadows.

This was no ordinary attack.

Ishan shook his head. "But that wasn't the worst part."

Shreyansh leaned forward. "What was?"

Ishan's eyes darkened. "When I looked down at the ruins, I saw him. Rudra. He was standing... alive. But he wasn't alone."

Shreyansh tensed. "Who was with him?"

"A man," Ishan whispered. "I don't know his name. But he was dressed in black, like a shadow. He stood beside Rudra, and behind them... a portal. A real, glowing
   portal."

The air in the room grew heavy.

"I screamed for Rudra," Ishan continued. "But he didn't look at me. He didn't even react. The man placed a hand on his shoulder, and then..."

He clenched his fists tighter, his nails digging into his palms. "They vanished."

Silence.

Shreyansh exhaled and ran a hand through his hair. "Damn..." He reached into his pocket and pulled out a
   small chocolate bar, tossing it to Ishan. "Here, eat this. It'll help calm you down."

Ishan stared at it blankly but didn't move.

Shreyansh stood up. "Wait here. I'll be back."

The Whispered Conversation

Stepping out of the room, Shreyansh closed the door behind him. In the dimly lit hallway, another ninja stood waiting—Varun.

Shreyansh exhaled sharply. "Varun, listen. The kid is terrified, but I got the full story."

Varun folded his arms. "Tell me."

Shreyansh glanced back at the closed door before continuing. "Rudra saved Ishan from getting crushed. But then something unnatural happened. His house didn't just get destroyed—it was erased. Like something wiped it off the face of the earth."

Varun's eyes narrowed. "And his brother?"

"Alive. But taken by a man named Dev. Whoever this Dev is, he didn't harm Ishan... but he took Rudra and left through a portal. That means we're dealing with something beyond our usual threats."

Varun's jaw tightened. "You think Dev planned this? That he destroyed the house just to take Rudra?"

Shreyansh nodded grimly. "It's possible. And it gets worse. There were three other people in that house when it exploded—Ishan's uncle, aunt... and their unborn child."

Varun's expression darkened. "So, not only was a child orphaned, but a full family was wiped out... except for
Rudra?"

"Exactly. Which means Dev didn't just pick randomly. He wanted Rudra. But why?"

Varun exhaled through his nose. "We need answers. Give me your notes—I'll report this to headquarters."

Shreyansh handed him a small notebook. "Take Ishan, too. The Guardians will want to see him. They need to check his full family background and determine why Dev took only Rudra and destroyed the rest."

Varun nodded. "Understood."

As he turned to leave, Shreyansh glanced back at the door.
   Poor kid... his life just turned into a nightmare.

And deep down, he knew... this was only the beginning.

After the whispered conversation, Varun stepped back into the dimly lit room, his sharp gaze landing on Ishan.

"Hello, Ishan. My name is Varun," he said, his voice firm yet calm. "We need to go. We're heading to headquarters."

Ishan, still shaken but curious, gave a slow nod. Without hesitation, Varun stepped forward and placed a strong yet gentle hand on the boy's shoulder.

"Hold on tight."

Varun's fingers shifted into a series of precise hand signs. Suddenly, his veins bulged beneath his skin, glowing faintly with energy. A surge of raw power pulsed through his legs, and in the blink of an eye, he was gone.

Arrival at the Headquarters

Within seconds, they reached the headquarters—a
 towering fortress hidden in the heart of the city. Its walls were made of
ancient stone, inscribed with mystical symbols that seemed to shift under the
moonlight. The air carried a strange energy, as if the very fabric of reality was
different here.

Ishan staggered slightly as they came to a stop, his mind reeling from the
sheer speed of their travel. "W-Whoa!" He gasped. "How did you do that?
That speed... Is magic
 real?"

Varun smirked. "I'll explain later." He motioned for Ishan to follow. "Come
on, we have more important things to do right now."

They entered the Grand Hall of the headquarters, where robed warriors and
scholars moved swiftly, their conversations hushed but purposeful. The walls
were adorned with ancient weapons, scrolls, and
 artifacts with unseen power.

Varun approached a young woman standing near the entrance. Her long silver
 hair shimmered under the soft glow of the torches, and her piercing blue eyes

flicked toward them with curiosity.

"Varun," she greeted, tilting her head slightly. "What brings you here in such a hurry?"

"We need to see the Elder Guardians. It's urgent."

She frowned. "They're in an important meeting. I can't just interrupt them."

"Please," Varun insisted. "It's a matter of life and death."

The woman hesitated before sighing. "Fine. But if I get in trouble for this, it's on you." She turned and slipped into the grand meeting hall, her footsteps silent.

Meeting the Elders

Inside the massive meeting room, five Elder Guardians sat around a circular stone table, their expressions grim. Each of them radiated an aura of unimaginable power. These were the most feared and respected warriors in the world of magic.

The young woman entered quietly, approaching the closest guardian and whispering in his ear.

The guardian frowned and turned to the others. "We have an emergency case. A boy named Ishan. He's here with
Varun."

The room fell silent. Then, one of the elders—an old man with silver hair and a scar across his eye—stood up.

"I already know why he's here," he said, his voice deep and commanding.

"Bring them in."

Varun and Ishan were led inside. The atmosphere was thick with power, and Ishan could feel the weight of unseen forces pressing down on him.

Varun stepped forward, handing a file to the elders. "This contains everything we've learned so far," he said. "Ishan's story, Rudra's disappearance, the man named Dev, and the destruction of his home."

The elders listened carefully, flipping through the reports.
   Then, the old man with silver hair slowly stood up again.

"I know everything," he said, his gaze locking onto Ishan's.

Ishan felt a chill run down his spine. "You... know everything?"

The elder nodded. "Yes. But before I tell you, I must speak to my grandson privately."

The room fell into stunned silence.

"Grandson?" Ishan repeated, his voice barely above a whisper.

The elder gave him a small, sad smile. "Yes, Ishan. I am Ravi—your grandfather."

The other elders exchanged glances but said nothing. One by one, they stood up and left the room, murmuring quoting themselves. Soon, only Ishan, Varun, and Ravi remained.

The Truth About Ishan's Family

Ravi gestured for Ishan to follow him into a separate chamber—a smaller room lined with books, old scrolls, and relics that radiated hidden energy. He closed the door behind them and turned to face his grandson.

"Sit," he said gently.

Ishan sat on a cushioned chair, his mind spinning. "Grandpa... I don't understand. You're my real
   grandfather?"

Ravi nodded. "Yes. And it's time you learned the truth about your family."
   Varun leaned against the wall, arms crossed, listening
   intently.

"Your father, Rahul, and your uncle, Rohan, were my greatest students," Ravi began. "They were both warriors of the Celestial Order, a secret group that protected humanity from supernatural threats."

Ishan's eyes widened. "Celestial Order? Supernatural threats? You mean... magic and monsters are real?"

Ravi smiled slightly. "Not just magic. There are creatures, demons, and even gods that walk among us, hidden from the normal world."

Ishan shivered. His whole life, he had believed magic was just fairy tales—but now, after everything he had seen, he wasn't so sure anymore.

Ravi continued. "Your father, Rahul, was one of the most powerful warriors of the Order. He had a special ability— one that only appears once in a generation."

Ishan leaned forward. "What kind of ability?"
  Ravi's expression turned serious. "The power of Divine Summoning."

Ishan blinked. "Divine... what?"

"Divine Summoning," Ravi repeated. "A rare gift that allows the user to call upon gods and celestial beings for power."

Ishan's breath caught in his throat. "My dad... could summon gods?"

"Yes. But with great power comes great danger." Ravi's face darkened. "There were those who feared him. Enemies who wanted his power for themselves. And that is
  why..."

He exhaled.

"That is why your parents were killed."

Silence filled the room.

Ishan felt like the floor had been ripped from under him.

"Killed? You mean... it wasn't an accident?"

"No," Ravi said. "It was murder. And I believe the same people who killed your father... are the ones who took
Rudra."

Ishan clenched his fists, his body trembling with rage and
grief.

"Who are they?" he demanded. "Who took my brother?"

Ravi met his eyes, his expression unreadable.

"They are called the Asura Clan."

Varun's expression hardened. "The Asuras... so they're involved?"

Ravi nodded. "And if Dev is working with them... then Rudra's fate may already be sealed."

Ishan gritted his teeth. "No. I won't let that happen."

Ravi placed a firm hand on his shoulder. "Then, my grandson, you must prepare yourself... because this is only the beginning."

Chapter 2: The History of the Past

The dim candlelight flickered as Ravi took a deep breath, his gaze locking onto Ishan's. "Listen carefully, my grandson," he began, his voice filled with the weight of centuries. "You must understand where you come from— where we come from—before you can truly grasp the war you are about to enter."

Ishan sat up straight, his heart pounding with anticipation.

Ravi continued, "Long ago, in the ancient times, there was a boy named Kabir. He was born into a family of priests, raised in devotion and meditation. His father, a great Sadhu, was deeply connected to the gods themselves. He was not just a man of faith—he was a seer, one who knew the very secrets of the universe."

Ishan frowned. "Secrets? What kind of secrets?"

Ravi's eyes darkened. "He knew how the world would end."

A heavy silence filled the room.

"He told Kabir everything," Ravi went on. "That after enlightenment, a person is given a choice—to enter the
Gates of Heaven or be condemned to the Depths of Hell. But... between those two gates lies something far more dangerous."

Ishan leaned forward. "What is it?"

"A thin passage—a void beyond human understanding," Ravi said. "And within that void lies three ropes. The Rope of Time, which governs all existence. The Rope of Heaven, which leads to divinity. And the Rope of Hell, which drags souls into the abyss."

Ishan shuddered. "And what happens if someone touches them?"

"Those who reach the Rope of Time can alter the course of reality itself," Ravi answered. "But hidden within it is something even more terrifying—an imaginary rope. A passage where dreams and reality intertwine. And one day, a boy will reach it... and when he does, the entire world will change."

A chill ran down Ishan's spine. "Change? How?"

Ravi's voice was grave. "That boy will awaken Asuras and Anti-Asuras, igniting a war so catastrophic that the world will drown in chaos. It will be a battle unlike any before—a fight that will bring only death and destruction."

Ishan clenched his fists. "Then what happened to Kabir?"

"He decided to become the one to protect the world," Ravi said. "He prayed, he meditated, and through sheer will, he gained enlightenment. With his newfound power, he traveled beyond the Gates of Heaven and Hell, stepping into the void. There, at the end of the imaginary line, he saw something that no one else had ever seen..."

Ishan's breath hitched. "What did he see?"

Ravi's expression darkened. "Nothing."

Ishan blinked. "Nothing?"

"Nothing. No one was sitting there. No god. No demon.
   Just emptiness."

Ishan felt a creeping unease settle over him.

Ravi exhaled. "Kabir realized then that time itself could never be changed. No one had ever controlled it before... and no one ever would. So, in an act of defiance, he summoned both Asuras and Anti-Asuras into reality. And in doing so, he... trapped himself inside the imaginary realm."

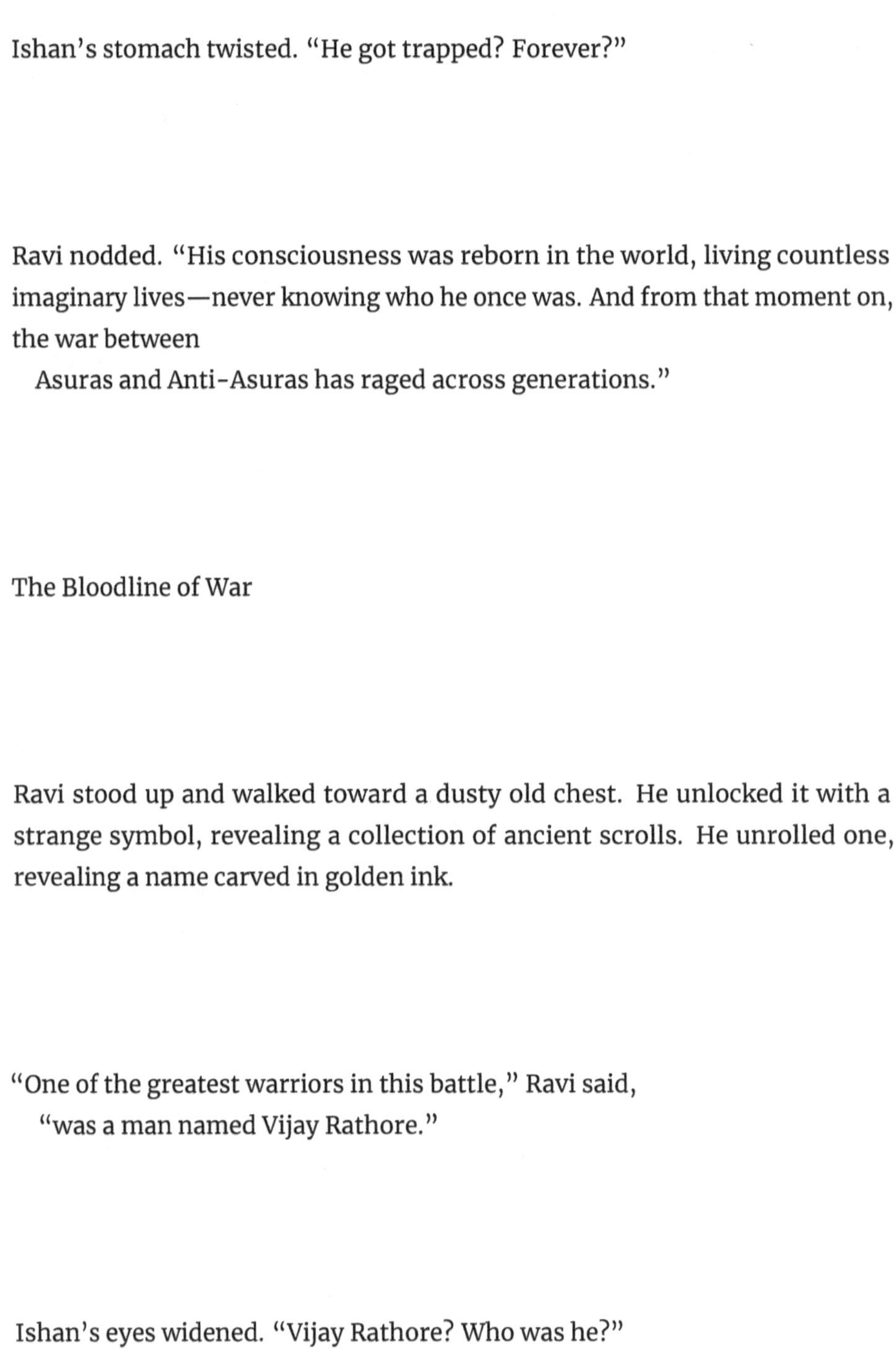

Ishan's stomach twisted. "He got trapped? Forever?"

Ravi nodded. "His consciousness was reborn in the world, living countless imaginary lives—never knowing who he once was. And from that moment on, the war between
Asuras and Anti-Asuras has raged across generations."

The Bloodline of War

Ravi stood up and walked toward a dusty old chest. He unlocked it with a strange symbol, revealing a collection of ancient scrolls. He unrolled one, revealing a name carved in golden ink.

"One of the greatest warriors in this battle," Ravi said,
"was a man named Vijay Rathore."

Ishan's eyes widened. "Vijay Rathore? Who was he?"

Ravi's voice was filled with pride. "He was my grandfather's grandfather. He was our ancestor. And he was so powerful that he once trapped the most feared demon inside his own soul."

Ishan's heart pounded. "He sealed a demon inside himself?"

"Not just any demon," Ravi corrected. "The world's most evil demon. A creature so vile that even the gods feared its existence. But Vijay knew that simply killing the demon wouldn't be enough. Instead, he locked the demon within himself and hid the key to its release in a mysterious place."

Ishan swallowed hard. "And what happened to him?"

Ravi's expression darkened. "During an Asura invasion, he knew the only way to protect the world was to take his own life. So, he did. He died with the demon still sealed within him... and to this day, no one knows where he hid the key."

Ishan's mind was spinning. "So... this war has been happening for generations?"

"Yes," Ravi confirmed. "And countless warriors—like your father—have died fighting in it."

Ishan's breath caught in his throat. "My father..."

Ravi placed a gentle hand on his shoulder. "That's why I erased your uncle's and aunt's memories. I told them I was just a government spy. I sent Rohan away so he could live a normal life, far from magic, far from war."

Ishan clenched his fists. "But now everything has changed. Dev took my brother. And I can't just sit here and do nothing."

Ravi's eyes met his. "So... what do you want to do?"

Ishan took a deep breath. "I understand everything now. I am a direct descendant of Vijay Rathore. And if this war is still happening, then I need to fight. I need to train, to get stronger... and most importantly, I need to save Rudra."

Ravi smiled, his old eyes gleaming with pride. "Then you are ready."

Ishan nodded. "Train me, Grandpa. Make me stronger."

Ravi stepped back, crossing his arms. "Very well. But know this—your training will not be easy. I will personally train you... along with others who, like you, are destined to fight in this war."

Ishan's heart pounded. "Other warriors?"

"Yes," Ravi said. "At Anti-Asura Academy, you will train alongside others who share your goal. There, you will unlock your true potential."

Ishan clenched his fists. "I'm ready."

Ravi nodded. "Then be prepared, my grandson. Because from this moment forward… your true journey begins."

The Path of an Anti-Asura

The Anti-Asura Academy was nothing like Ishan had imagined. It was a fortress hidden deep within the mountains, its dark stone walls etched with glowing symbols. Massive iron gates stood tall, guarded by warriors in jet-black armor, their faces hidden behind eerie, skull like masks.

As Varun led Ishan through the entrance, a sharp chill ran down his spine. This was a place of warriors—a
 battleground where only the strong survived.

Inside, the academy was a strange mix of tradition and brutality. The main hall had towering statues of legendary warriors, their swords raised toward the heavens. Beyond it, training grounds stretched far and wide, filled with students battling against one another or meditating under the cold gaze of their instructors.

Ishan noticed the stares almost instantly.

Some students whispered, others glared. The weight of their eyes pressed down on him, their resentment almost suffocating.

"That's the Elder grandson?" one voice
  sneered.
  "Of course, they gave him special treatment."
  "He'll probably get stronger without even trying."

Ishan clenched his fists. He had done nothing, yet they already hated him.

The Teachers & the First Lesson

Varun led him into a grand hall where a few instructors stood waiting. The most striking figure among them was

Sahil Saxena—a tall, lean man with sharp eyes that carried both wisdom and sorrow. His long black coat fluttered as he approached Ishan, his expression unreadable.

"Ishan Rathore," he said, his voice even. "I've heard about you."

Ishan swallowed hard.

"You don't need to prove yourself to me," Sahil continued. "But if you wish to survive in this world, you must become more than just the grandson of an Elder Guardian. You must become a warrior."

The first lesson began immediately.

The training grounds were brutal. Students were made to fight in one-on-one duels, pushed beyond exhaustion, and forced to endure grueling physical

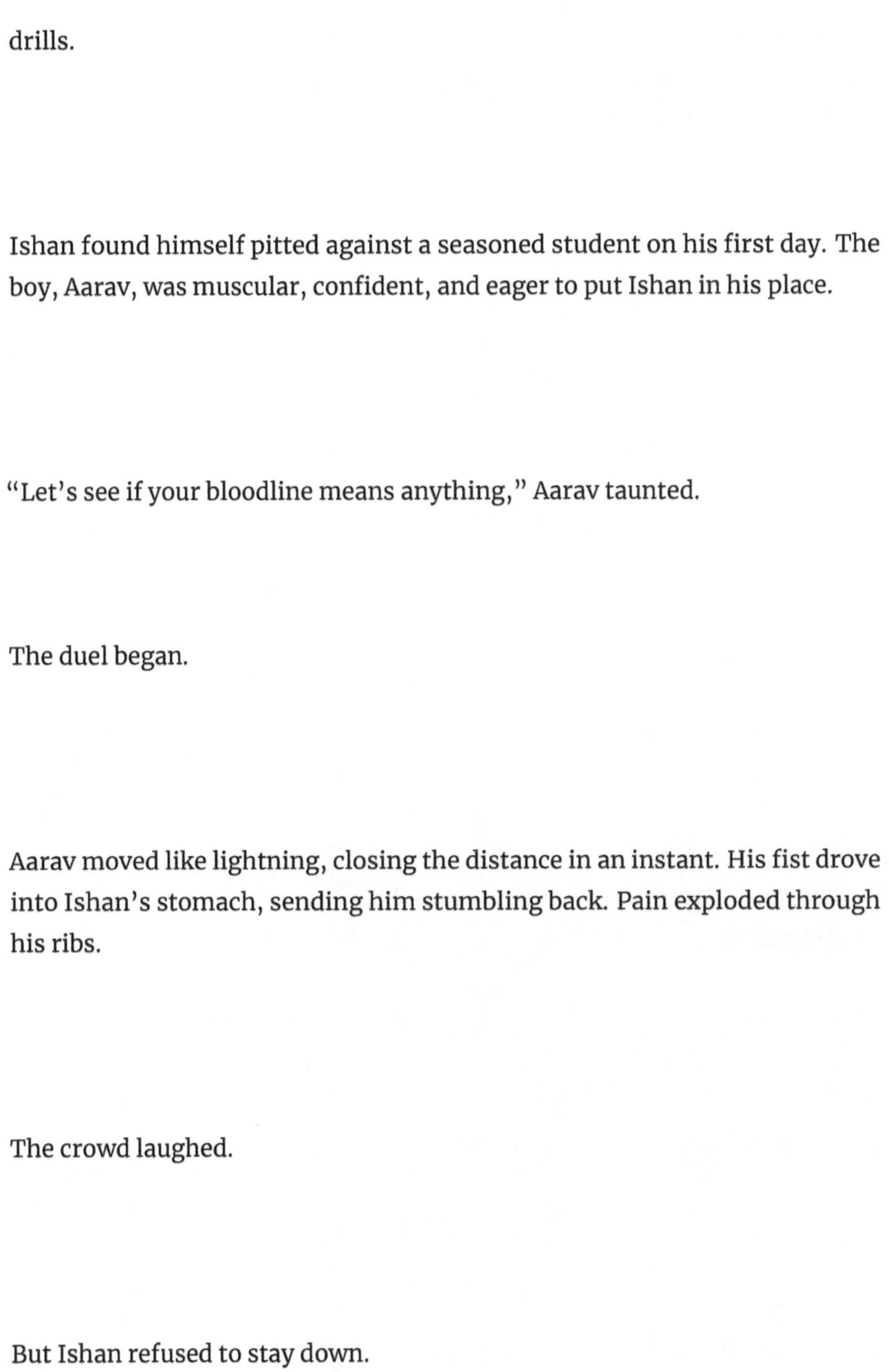

drills.

Ishan found himself pitted against a seasoned student on his first day. The boy, Aarav, was muscular, confident, and eager to put Ishan in his place.

"Let's see if your bloodline means anything," Aarav taunted.

The duel began.

Aarav moved like lightning, closing the distance in an instant. His fist drove into Ishan's stomach, sending him stumbling back. Pain exploded through his ribs.

The crowd laughed.

But Ishan refused to stay down.

He charged forward, dodging a second blow by instinct alone. His body moved faster than he thought possible, his reflexes sharpening. For the first time, he realized—he was changing.

Breaking Limits

The training continued for weeks.

Ishan's body adapted, his muscles growing stronger, his speed increasing. He pushed himself relentlessly, running until his lungs burned, fighting until his knuckles bled.

Slowly, he surpassed his classmates.

His punches became faster than the eye could follow.

His endurance became inhuman, allowing him to fight for hours.

His reflexes became sharp enough to dodge attacks with ease.

Yet, his peers only grew more resentful.

His closest friend, Raghav, once the only person who supported him, began to distance himself.

"You don't even need to try," Raghav muttered one night.
   "You're already special."

The betrayal stung.

Ishan realized then—he was truly alone.

The First Encounter with an Asura

One night, as the students trained in the outer grounds, a scream pierced the air.

A monstrous shadow leaped from the treetops, its form twisting and shifting. Red eyes glowed in the darkness—an Asura had breached the academy's barriers.

Before the instructors could react, the creature lunged toward the nearest student.

Ishan didn't think.
   His body moved on instinct, launching forward at full speed. He grabbed the student and shoved him aside just as the Asura's claws tore through the air.

The beast snarled, its serpentine body coiling like a demon from a nightmare.

The students scattered in fear.

49

But Ishan stood his ground.

This was his fight.

The Asura attacked, its claws aimed for his throat. Ishan ducked at the last second, twisting his body like a shadow, and countered with a devastating punch to its ribs.

The impact sent shock waves through the air.

The beast reeled, but it wasn't enough.

It lunged again, faster—too fast.

Ishan braced himself—but then a blur of motion

intercepted the attack.

Sahil Saxena had arrived.

His sword gleamed in the moonlight as he effortlessly sliced through the Asura, its body disintegrating into ash.

Ishan stared, his heart hammering.

"That," Sahil said, turning to him, "is the power you must achieve."

A Dark Presence Watches

Unknown to them, far beyond the academy, someone was watching.

Dev sat within a darkened chamber, his hand resting on the unconscious body of Rudra. Around him, runes of ancient power flickered, binding Rudra in chains of darkness.

One of his spies kneel-ed before him.

"It is confirmed, Lord Dev," the spy said. "The boy, Ishan
    Rathore... He is growing stronger."

Dev smirked.

"Good," he whispered. "Let him grow. The stronger he becomes... the sweeter
it will be when I take everything from him."

His fingers tightened around Rudra's forehead, and the room was filled with
the sound of a tortured scream.

Chapter 3: The Forge of Strength

Ishan had never trained like this before.

The Anti-Asura Academy didn't believe in half-measures. Their philosophy was simple—break the body, rebuild it stronger.

The training grounds stretched endlessly, filled with students pushing themselves beyond human limits. The air reeked of sweat and blood, the ground was stained with the exhaustion of warriors who refused to quit.

And now, it was Ishan's turn.

The First Trial: The Unforgiving Morning

Before sunrise, Ishan was dragged from his bed.

His instructor for physical conditioning, Master Arvind, stood before him—a man built like a statue, his muscles carved from years of relentless discipline.

"Weakness," Arvind said, "is a disease. And today, we burn it out of you."

The first task was simple: run.

5 kilometers. Barefoot. On rocky terrain.

The ground cut into Ishan's feet, each step sending sharp pain through his legs. He wanted to stop—but every time he slowed, Arvind cracked a whip against the dirt behind him.

"Move faster, Rathore! Or I'll feed you to the Asuras myself!"

By the time Ishan reached the end, his legs trembled, his breath ragged. But this was just the beginning.

The Second Trial: The Thousand Repetitions

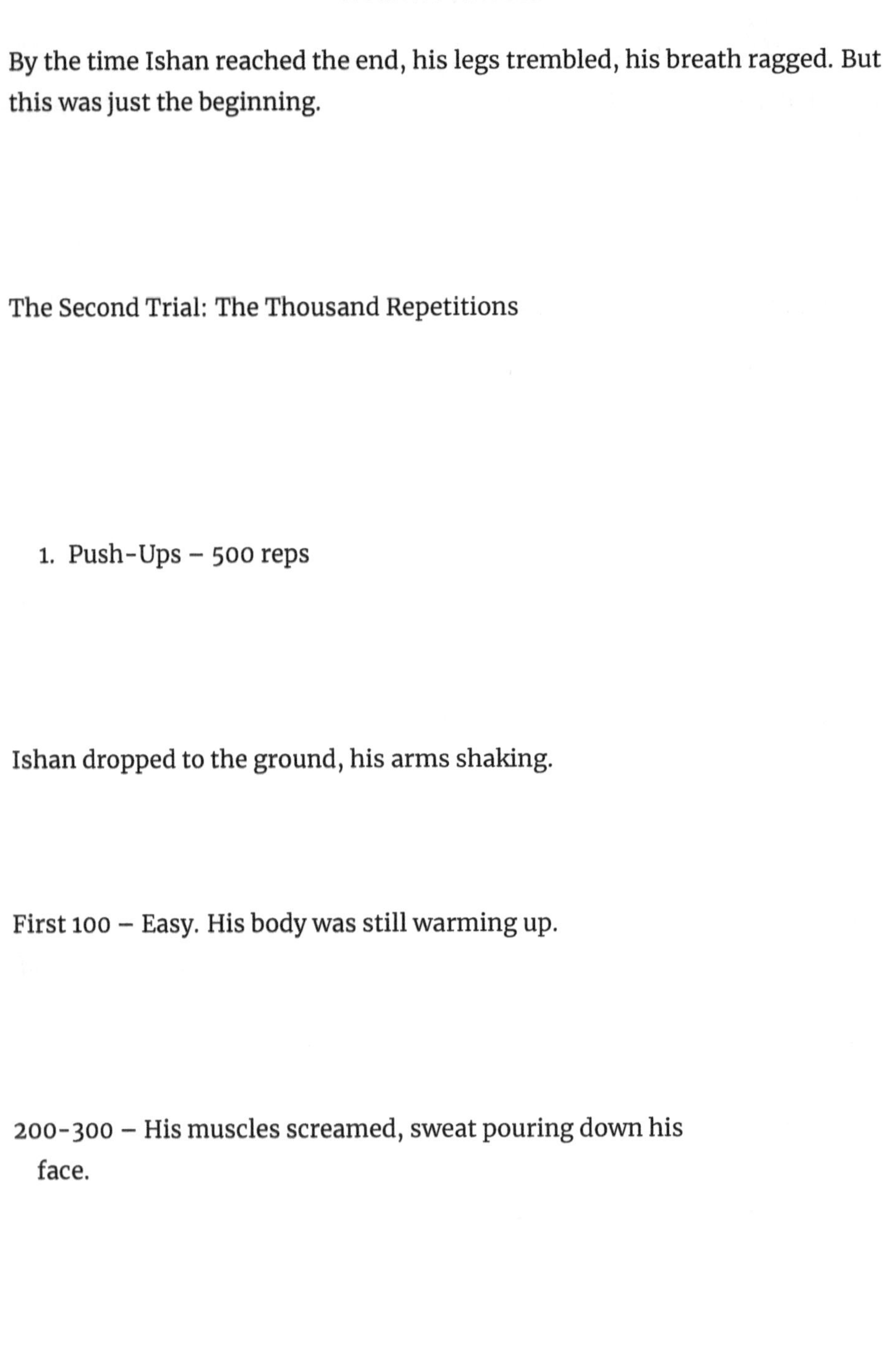

1. Push-Ups – 500 reps

Ishan dropped to the ground, his arms shaking.

First 100 – Easy. His body was still warming up.

200-300 – His muscles screamed, sweat pouring down his face.

400-500 – His arms barely moved. His chest burned, his body on the verge of collapse.

But stopping was not an option.

1. Crunches – 300 reps

Each crunch felt like knives stabbing his abdomen. His core tightened with every movement, sweat dripping from his forehead.

1. Sit-Ups – 300 reps

Every rep sent fire through his stomach. His breathing became shallow, but he clenched his teeth and pushed through.

1. Squats – 500 reps

His thighs burned like molten lava. With each squat, his legs shook violently.

1. Burpees – 200 reps

Each burpee felt like a death sentence. His lungs gasped for air, his heart pounded in his chest.

1. Plank – 10 minutes

The longest ten minutes of his life.

His arms quivered, his core felt like it would shatter. But he refused to collapse.

The Breaking Point

By noon, Ishan's body had shut down.

He collapsed onto the dirt, his limbs refusing to move. His mind screamed at him to stop.

But then, Master Arvind knelt beside him.

"Your father didn't stop."

Ishan's eyes snapped open.

"Your grandfather didn't stop."

He gritted his teeth, his fists clenched.

"Get. Up."

With a primal roar, Ishan forced himself onto his feet.

His body was broken. But his spirit was not.

Beyond Human Limits

As days turned into weeks, Ishan's body transformed.

His arms became steel, his punches carrying enough force to crack stone.

His legs became unyielding, able to sprint faster and jump higher than ever before."

His core became a fortress, his endurance reaching superhuman levels.

The students who once mocked him now watched in awe.

Ishan Rathore was no longer just the grandson of an Elder Guardian.

He was becoming something far more terrifying.

The Awakening of Power

Ishan's body had been forged in fire. Now, it was time to forge his spirit.

The Anti-Asura Academy had two types of warriors—those who relied on pure physical strength, and those who mastered the mystic arts.

Ishan was expected to master both.

His magic instructor, Professor Aarav Tiwari, stood before him in the training chamber. Unlike the brutal Master Arvind, Aarav was calm and calculated—his eyes sharp, his aura pulsing with energy.

"Magic is not just power," Aarav said. "It is will. It is focus. It is the force that binds the universe itself."

Ishan listened carefully, his heart racing.

Today, he would step into a world beyond human comprehension.

Step One: Releasing Internal Energy

Aarav had Ishan sit in the center of a dimly lit hall, surrounded by candles.

"Close your eyes," he instructed. "Feel your breath. Feel your heartbeat."

Ishan obeyed.

Thump-thump. Thump-thump.

His breathing slowed. He focused inward.

"Now," Aarav continued, "visualize your energy. Imagine it like a flame inside you."

At first, there was nothing. Just darkness.

Then—a spark.

A warmth spread through Ishan's chest, tingling in his veins. He gasped.

"Good," Aarav said. "Now, let it flow."

Ishan concentrated. The energy moved, coursing through his arms, his legs—his very soul.

Suddenly, his fingers flickered with a golden glow. His eyes widened.

He could feel the energy inside him, pulsing like a second heartbeat.

This was his power.

Step Two: Transforming Energy into Physical Form "Releasing energy is easy," Aarav said. "Shaping it—that's the real challenge."

Ishan held out his hand. Golden energy swirled at his fingertips, but it was unstable—wild, chaotic.

"Concentrate," Aarav urged. "Give it form."

Ishan imagined a blade.

The energy flickered. It began to stretch—shimmering, shifting—until finally—

A dagger of pure light materialized in his palm.

Ishan gasped. It felt solid. Real.

Aarav smirked. "Not bad. Now, let's make it bigger."

Step Three: Infusing Objects with Energy

Aarav tossed a wooden stick to Ishan.

"Now, channel your energy into this."

Ishan gripped the stick. At first, nothing happened.

"Don't force it. Feel the object. Let your energy seep into it."

Ishan focused. His energy flowed from his palm, sinking into the wood.

The stick began to glow faintly, vibrating with power.

Aarav nodded. "Now, imagine it as a weapon."

The stick hardened, its edges sharpening. In seconds, it had transformed into a steel rod, buzzing with raw energy.

Ishan's jaw dropped. "I... I did that?"

Aarav chuckled. "You did. Now, try something smaller."

Ishan picked up a pen. He poured energy into it—his focus sharper this time.

The pen's tip extended, turning into a needle-thin dagger.

Aarav's smile widened. "You're learning fast."

Step Four: The First Combat Test

No training was complete without a fight.

Aarav snapped his fingers.

From the shadows, two low-level Asuras emerged—
snarling, their monstrous eyes locked on Ishan.

"Your task?" Aarav said. "Take them down."

Ishan clenched his fists. He was ready.

The first Asura lunged. Ishan sidestepped, energy surging through him.

He grabbed a wooden staff—infused it with power—and swung. The Asura was sent flying, crashing into the wall.

The second Asura charged. Ishan formed a dagger of energy and slashed. The blade sliced through its arm like butter.

The creatures howled, vanishing into dust.

Ishan stood there, panting, victorious.

Aarav crossed his arms. "Not bad. But this is only the beginning."

Chapter 4: The Secrets of the Ancestors

Ishan sat on the cold stone floor of his training room, drenched in sweat. His muscles ached, his body screamed for rest, and his mind felt like it was on the verge of breaking. No matter how much he trained, it felt like he was barely scratching the surface of his potential. He had spent weeks pushing his limits, yet the power he sought
still felt distant, just out of reach.

Frustrated, he stormed into his grandfather Ravi's chamber, finding the old man seated cross-legged, reading an ancient manuscript. "Grandpa, there has to be an easier way," Ishan blurted out. "A shortcut—some trick to mastering all this faster. You're the elder guardian. You must know something."

Ravi slowly closed his book and looked at Ishan with knowing eyes. "You think power comes easily, boy?" His voice was calm but carried a weight that made Ishan hesitate. "The path to strength has no shortcuts. The more you train, the stronger you become. That is the only truth."

Ishan clenched his fists. "But Dev—he's already powerful! If I don't grow stronger quickly, I won't stand a chance against him. I need something more!"

Ravi sighed, then stood up. "If you seek true power, then come with me."

The Hidden Cave of the Ancestors

Ishan followed his grandfather through a dark passage that twisted deep beneath the academy. The air grew colder, and an eerie silence filled the tunnel. They stopped before an ancient stone wall, covered in inscriptions glowing faintly in the darkness.

Ravi placed his palm on one of the stones, and the entire wall trembled before slowly splitting apart. Behind it lay a vast underground cavern. Torches ignited along the walls as they stepped inside, revealing a breathtaking sight— a chamber filled with the legacy of Ishan's ancestors.

Weapons of all kinds lined the walls—kunai, swords, chains, ninja stars, magical rods, and special armor that had been passed down through generations. Ancient scrolls and books were stacked neatly on stone shelves, holding knowledge lost to time.

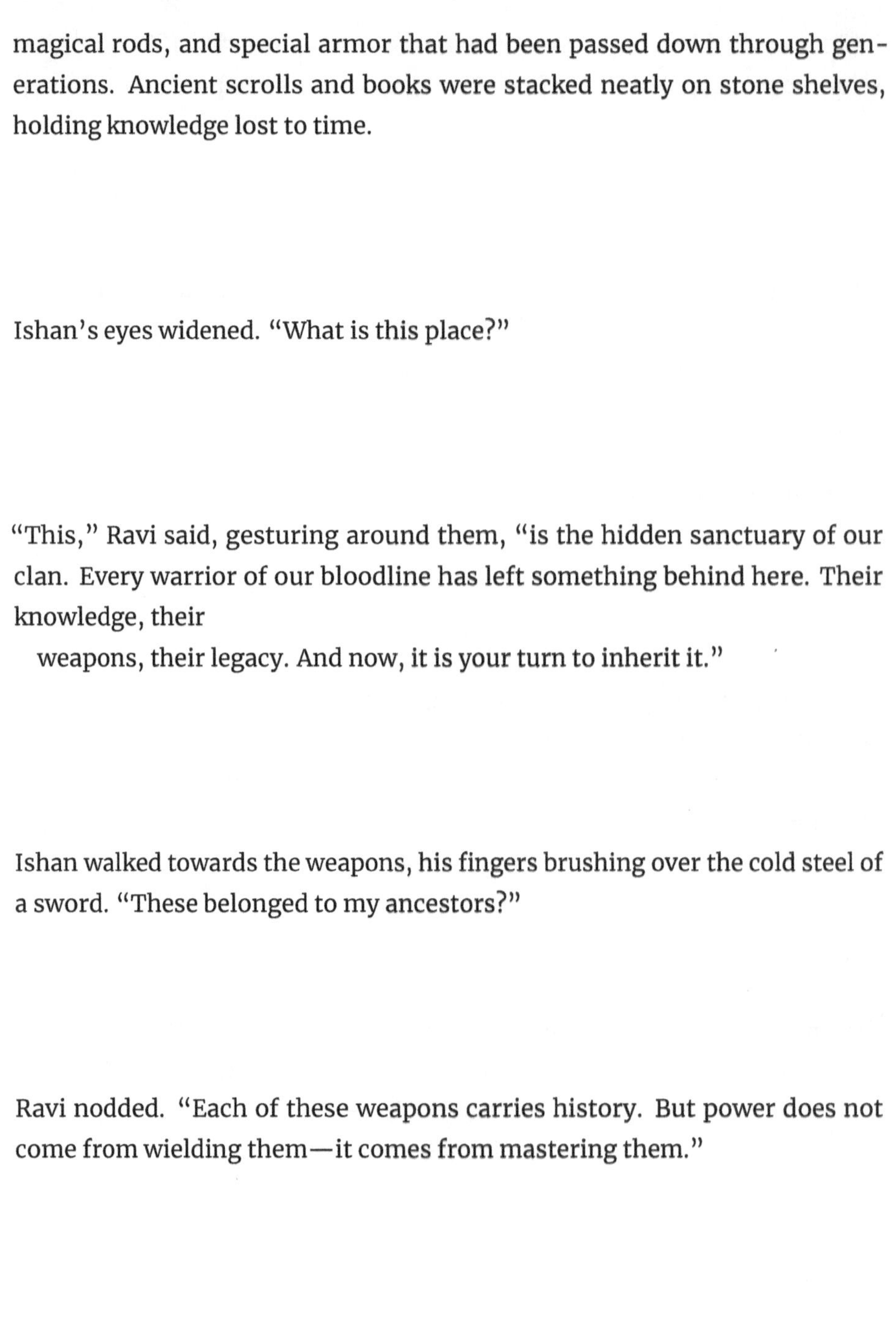

Ishan's eyes widened. "What is this place?"

"This," Ravi said, gesturing around them, "is the hidden sanctuary of our clan. Every warrior of our bloodline has left something behind here. Their knowledge, their
  weapons, their legacy. And now, it is your turn to inherit it."

Ishan walked towards the weapons, his fingers brushing over the cold steel of a sword. "These belonged to my ancestors?"

Ravi nodded. "Each of these weapons carries history. But power does not come from wielding them—it comes from mastering them."

The True Power of His Clan

Ravi stepped forward and raised his hand. A faint glow appeared around his palm, and suddenly, a wisp of energy floated into the air—pure, concentrated soul energy. It swirled like a flame, casting strange shadows on the cave walls.

"Our clan has a power unlike any other," Ravi said. "The ability to catch, destroy, absorb, or control souls. That is our birthright, passed down from our ancestor, Vijay
Rathore."

Ishan's breath caught in his throat. "Control souls?"

"Yes," Ravi said gravely. "It is an ability feared by even the strongest Asuras. Your father had this power. And one day, so will you."

Ishan's mind raced. This was more than just physical or magical strength—it was something greater, something terrifying. "If this is our clan's power, why was it kept a secret?"

"Because it is dangerous," Ravi said. "It requires immense control. If misused, it can corrupt even the strongest of men. That is why only those who are worthy may learn it."

Ishan took a deep breath. "Then I will learn it."

A New Training Begins

Ravi smiled. "Good. But first, you must be tested. No more easy training. From now on, you will train in this cave every day. Here, your body, mind, and soul will be pushed beyond their limits."

Ishan nodded, determination burning in his eyes.

Ravi gestured to the books lining the walls. "And before you learn to control souls, you will study. These books contain secrets on obtaining special abilities. Read them, understand them. Knowledge is just as important as strength."

Ishan looked at the shelves, knowing that his real journey had just begun. He had come here looking for shortcuts, but he now understood—there were none. Only training would make him worthy.

With a deep breath, he reached for the first book and opened it, ready to embrace his destiny.

The Path to Becoming a Ninja

Ishan sat cross-legged in front of a stack of ancient books, their covers worn with age. Dust swirled in the dim light of the torches flickering along the walls of the hidden cave. His grandfather had told him that the knowledge contained within these pages held the secrets of his ancestors—their techniques, their strategies, and the hand signs required to channel his power efficiently.

His fingers traced the old Sanskrit-like inscriptions as he carefully opened the first book. The pages were filled with detailed illustrations of combat techniques, energy flow manipulation, and forbidden arts that had been passed down for generations. Some techniques required immense focus, while others demanded raw physical strength.

Learning the Ancient Techniques

Each book contained a new discovery. Some described powerful martial arts techniques, while others detailed the secrets of manipulating soul energy, fire, water, and even lightning. Ishan's mind raced as he absorbed every word.

Vayu Hast Mudra (Wind Hand Sign): Allowed him to move at extreme speeds, almost like a blur.

Agni Hasta (Fire Hand Sign): Let him release bursts of flame from his palms.

Astra Hasta (Weapon Transfer Sign): A method to transfer his energy into objects like kunai, swords, and even small pins, making them indestructible.

Shakti Drishti (Energy Vision): A way to sense opponents' movements even in complete darkness.

After hours of reading, Ishan stood up and began practicing the hand signs in the center of the cave. He started slow, carefully forming each symbol with his fingers, feeling the flow of energy inside him. At first, the techniques were unstable. Lightning crackled weakly in his palms, flames flickered for only a moment before dying out. But he didn't stop. He repeated each sign over and over until his movements were flawless.

Physical Training Inside the Cave

Ishan's body had already undergone significant changes, but now he intensified his training further.

Every day, he pushed himself harder than before:

500 push-ups

500 sit-ups

500 squats

500 leg raises

Pull-ups hanging from cave rocks

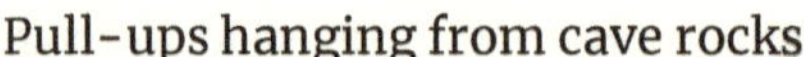

Balancing on kunai blades with one foot He practiced weapon combat, slashing at stone dummies with swords, throwing ninja stars at moving targets, and using chains to disarm enemies in mock battles. His body hardened under the relentless strain, his endurance increasing beyond human limits.

The Hidden Waterfall & Mental Training

One day, while exploring the deeper parts of the cave, Ishan discovered a hidden waterfall. The water flowed from a crack in the ceiling, cascading into a small underground lake. The sound of the rushing water was deafening, yet calming at the same time.

Ravi had once told him that true warriors trained both body and mind. So, Ishan sat under the freezing waterfall, letting the water crash onto his shoulders.

He focused on his breathing, his heart rate slowing, his mind sharpening. Meditation became part of his daily routine—blocking out distractions, enhancing his focus, and strengthening his ability to channel energy without wasting it.

Fighting Demons & Becoming a True Ninja

As the months passed, demons began appearing inside the cave. These creatures were weaker than the high-level Asuras but still deadly.

At first, Ishan struggled. Some demons were faster than him. Others had thick skin that his kunai couldn't pierce. But he adapted. He dodged faster, struck with precision, and learned to predict their movements using his growing battle instincts.

By the time he turned twelve, he had killed over 30 demons.

His muscles were sharp and defined. His reflexes were inhumanly fast. His energy control was nearing mastery.

Yet, despite everything, he still wasn't officially a ninja.

The Final Test

One night, as Ishan sat in front of the waterfall, Ravi appeared before him.

"You've grown strong," his grandfather said, his voice filled with pride. "But strength alone does not make you a ninja.

You need recognition."

Ishan stood up, clenching his fists. "Then tell me—how do I become a true ninja?"

Ravi smiled. "Defeat me in battle."

Ishan's heart pounded. He knew how powerful his
grandfather was. But this was the final test. This was his chance to prove
himself.

With determination in his eyes, Ishan took his stance, ready to face his greatest
challenge yet.

Chapter 5: The Grandfather's Trial and the Warrior's Path

The air in the hidden cave grew tense as Ishan stood before his grandfather, Ravi Rathore, ready to prove himself. The torches along the walls flickered as if sensing the battle that was about to begin. Ishan's muscles tensed, his grip on his kunai tightening.

Ravi stood calmly, his arms folded behind his back. "Show me everything you've learned," he said, his voice steady.

"If you can defeat me, you will earn the title of Ninja." Ishan charged forward with blinding speed, throwing a series of kunai infused with his energy. Ravi dodged effortlessly, moving as if time itself bent around him.

The Battle Begins

Ishan closed the distance in an instant, aiming a powerful roundhouse kick at Ravi's chest. But his grandfather caught his leg mid-air and tossed him aside with ease.

Ishan flipped mid-air and landed gracefully.

"Too slow," Ravi said.

Ishan gritted his teeth and formed the Agni Hasta (Fire Hand Sign), launching a wave of flames. Ravi countered by raising a single hand, absorbing the fire into his palm before extinguishing it with a flick of his fingers.

Not giving up, Ishan weaved through multiple hand signs in rapid succession, summoning chains infused with his energy. The chains wrapped around Ravi's arm, tightening with force.

But Ravi vanished in a blink.

Before Ishan could react, a fist struck his stomach with such force that the cave walls cracked. He flew backward, coughing blood, but rolled to his feet immediately.

"You're still holding back," Ravi said, his voice firm but patient.

Ishan wiped his mouth. He knew his grandfather wasn't using his full power. If he wanted to win, he had to go all out.

Awakening the Hidden Power

Ishan closed his eyes, focusing deep within himself. His aura flared, his energy bursting out like a storm. His body felt lighter, his mind sharper. The training he had endured, the battles he had fought—it all led to this moment.

When he opened his eyes again, they shimmered with a
  faint glow.

In an instant, Ishan vanished from sight.

This time, it was Ravi who was forced to defend. Ishan appeared behind him, launching a flurry of kicks and punches. Each strike carried the weight of his full strength.

His speed was overwhelming, his reflexes faster than ever.

For the first time, Ravi stepped back.

Taking advantage of the moment, Ishan performed his most powerful technique yet—Shakti Drishti (Energy Vision). With his enhanced perception, he predicted Ravi's movements before they even happened.

He lunged forward with a kunai infused with all his remaining energy.

Ravi raised his hand to block, but at the last second, Ishan changed his trajectory, spinning mid-air and landing a direct strike to Ravi's back.

The impact sent Ravi skidding across the cave floor.

For a moment, there was silence. Then, Ravi chuckled and stood up, dusting himself off. His eyes gleamed with pride.

"Well done," he said. "You win."

Ishan fell to his knees, breathing heavily. His entire body ached, but a smile spread across his face. He had done it. "You are now a Ninja," Ravi declared.

The Ranks of Power

After the battle, Ravi led Ishan deeper into the cave. He showed him an ancient wall engraving, depicting four ranks of warriors:

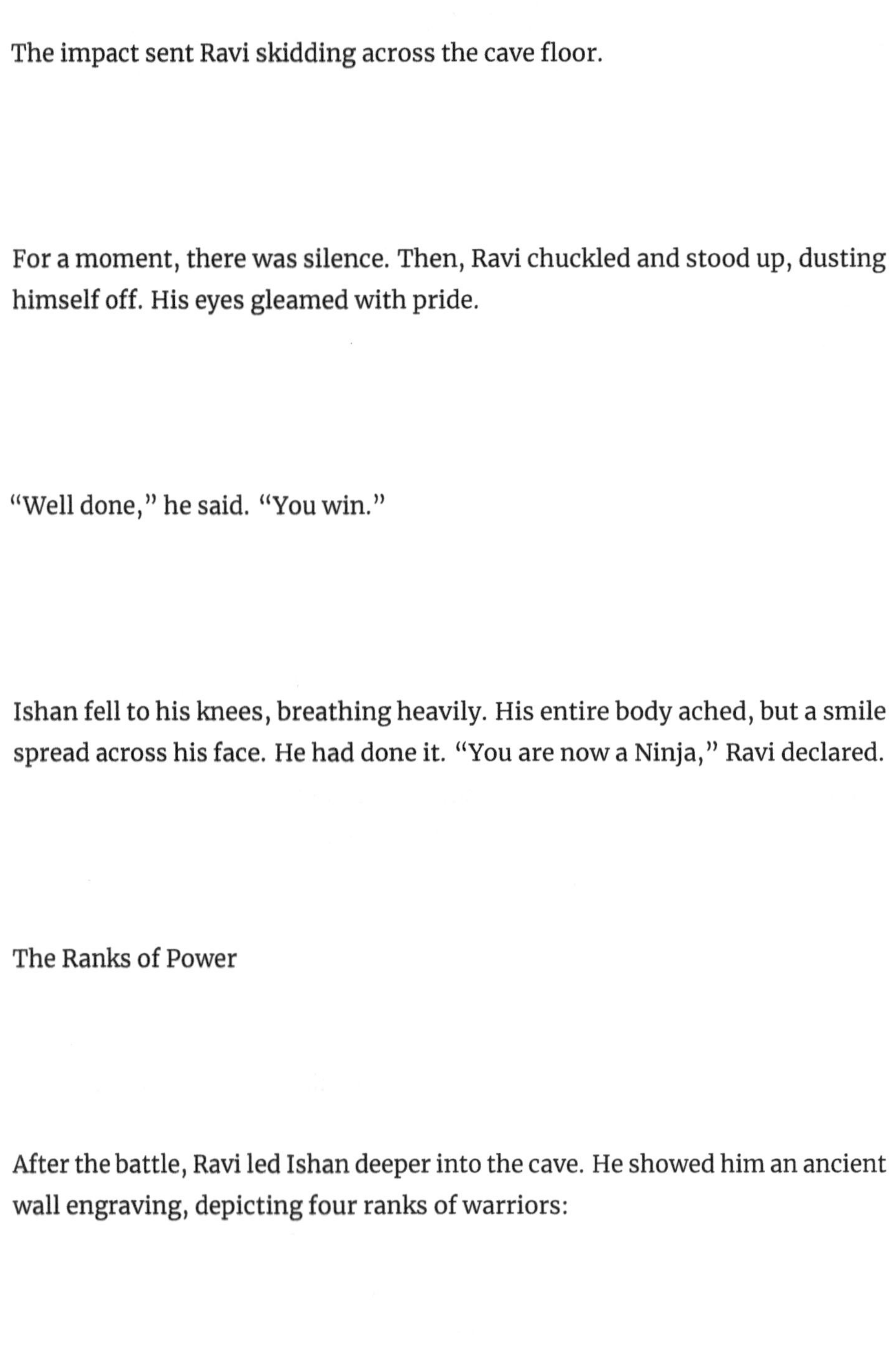

1. Ninja – The first step, earned through battle and skill.
2. Warrior – A higher level, where one must prove themselves in battle against others.
3. Elder Guardian – Those who protect the balance between Asuras and Anti-Asuras.
4. Yodha – The supreme rank, achieved only by the strongest of warriors, who command armies and lead great battles.

"You are now a Ninja, but your journey has just begun,"

Ravi said. "Your next goal is to become a Warrior."

Ishan's eyes burned with determination.

The Anti-Asura Warrior Exam

That night, as Ishan rested, a meeting was held among the Elder Guardians.

Seated in a grand chamber, the Guardians discussed the upcoming Anti-Asura Warrior Exam—an event where the strongest young fighters from all over the world would gather in India to compete. The winner would be
recognized as a true Warrior.

One of the Guardians spoke, "With the recent rise in Asura activity, we must ensure that only the strongest warriors ascend in rank. This year's exam will be the most
challenging yet."

Another Guardian added, "Dev's forces are growing. We must prepare our next generation for the battle ahead."

Ravi, seated among them, nodded. "I have already chosen my candidate."
The Guardians turned to him.

"My grandson, Ishan Rathore."

The room fell silent for a moment before the head Guardian spoke.

"Then it is decided. The Anti-Asura Warrior Exam will be held in one month."

Ishan's Next Challenge Begins

The next morning, Ravi summoned Ishan and informed him of the upcoming exam.

"In one month, you will face warriors from all over the world. This will be your chance to prove your strength and earn the title of Warrior."

Ishan clenched his fists. He had trained harder than ever, endured pain beyond measure. But this was just the beginning.

With his new goal set, Ishan prepared himself for the most intense battle of his life.

The Awakening of Infinite Eyes

The Path to the Exam

Ishan approached Sahil Saxena, one of the most respected teachers at the Anti-Asura Academy. He bowed slightly before handing him a form for the upcoming Warrior Exam.

Sahil took the form, glanced over it, and nodded. "So, you're finally ready?"

"Yes, Sir." Ishan's voice was steady.

Sahil smiled. "Good. Come with me, we need to submit this at the headquarters."

The two left the academy and traveled toward the Elder
   Guardian Headquarters, passing through a dense jungle.
   The air was thick with silence, but something felt... off.

Suddenly, the wind shifted.
   A chilling killing intent filled the air.

Sahil immediately stopped, his sharp eyes scanning the surroundings. "Ishan, stay behind me," he ordered.

Before Ishan could ask anything, a high-level Asura appeared from the shadows.

The creature stood tall, with jet-black skin, piercing red eyes, and razor-sharp claws. Its aura was suffocating, thick with malice.

"An Anti-Asura teacher, how interesting," the Asura sneered. "You will make a fine corpse."

The Battle Begins

Without warning, the Asura lunged at Sahil, claws extended. Sahil countered instantly, summoning a golden energy barrier. The Asura's claws screeched against it, but it did not break.

Sahil's hands moved in a blur, forming hand signs. "Agni Hasta—Inferno Strike!"

A massive pillar of fire erupted from his palms, engulfing the Asura. The creature roared in pain but emerged from the flames, completely unscathed.

"Pathetic."

It raised its hand, summoning four more Asuras from the shadows.

Sahil's face darkened. "Damn it. Ishan, don't move."

The battle turned chaotic. Sahil fought fiercely, using fire, lightning, and wind magic, dodging deadly attacks. But the Asuras were relentless.

Then—a sharp claw slashed through Sahil's side.

Blood sprayed into the air.

Sahil staggered back, clutching his wound. His breathing grew heavy. The Asuras took the opportunity and rained down blows upon him, beating him mercilessly.

Ishan watched in horror as his teacher fell to his knees, coughing blood.

Something inside him snapped.

The Awakening of Infinite Eyes

A dark, ominous aura exploded from Ishan's body. The jungle itself seemed to tremble.

The Asuras took a step back. For the first time, they felt
 fear.

Ishan's body pulsed with energy, his veins glowing. His normally dark eyes transformed—a three-legged fan-like energy design appeared in his pupils.

He had awakened his clan's legendary ability—The Infinite Eyes.

A void tore open around him, an endless dark abyss swallowing everything.

"This is…" one of the Asuras stuttered.

"The Void Dimension."

Total Annihilation

The moment the Asuras looked into Ishan's eyes, they were trapped inside his domain.

Inside the Void Dimension, time and space became meaningless. Ishan stood as the absolute ruler.

The Asuras screamed in terror as their souls were forcibly extracted from their bodies.

Ishan absorbed their energy, feeling their power merge with his own.

Then—he clenched his fist.

With a single punch, he obliterated their physical forms, leaving nothing but dust.

The last remaining high-level Asura roared in fury. "You little brat! I'll destroy you—"

Ishan's eyes glowed.

The Asura froze in place, completely powerless.

"You don't belong in this world," Ishan said coldly.

With one final gaze, he erased the Asura's soul from existence.

The Aftermath

As the battle ended, Ishan's dangerous aura faded. His face remained calm but deadly serious.

He turned and picked up his injured teacher. In the next instant, he vanished, moving at lightning speed toward the hospital.

Meanwhile... in the Asura's Domain

In a dark fortress, the remaining Asuras gathered before their lord—Dev.

A trembling Asura kneel-ed before him.

"My Lord... the one who killed our warriors... his name is
  Ishan Rathore."

Dev leaned forward, smirking. "Oh? So the boy has finally awakened his clan's power?"

The Asura nodded, sweating in fear. "Yes, my Lord. His eyes... they are terrifying. He erased our warriors in an instant."

Dev chuckled darkly. "Interesting."

Another Asura spoke, "Lord Dev, the Warrior Exam is in one month. Many Anti-Asuras will gather there. It's the perfect opportunity."

A sinister grin spread across Dev's face.

"Then let's crash their little event."

He stood up, his malicious aura shaking the entire fortress.

"In one month, we will annihilate the Anti-Asura world."

His laughter echoed in the halls. The Asuras joined in, their demonic laughter filling the darkness.

Chapter 6: The Meeting for the Warrior Exam

The hospital was quiet, except for the faint beeping of machines and the occasional footsteps of nurses. Ishan sat beside Sahil Sir's bed, watching the steady rise and fall of his chest. The battle in the jungle replayed in his mind— the moment his Infinity Eyes awakened, the overwhelming power surging through him, and the way the Asura had crumbled before him.

He flexed his fingers, still feeling the remnants of that energy. What is this power? How far can I push it?

The door creaked open. Elder Guardian Ravi entered, followed by several students who had come to check on Sahil Sir. Ravi's sharp eyes scanned the room before settling on Ishan.

"You did well," Ravi said, stepping closer. "Sahil Sir is alive because of you."

Ishan nodded but hesitated. "Sir, I need to tell you something."

Ravi crossed his arms. "Go on."

Ishan took a deep breath. "During the fight, something... changed in me. My eyes—they became something else.
    They unlocked a power I've never felt before."

Ravi's expression remained unreadable. "Describe it."

"I was surrounded by ten Asuras. One of them—the
    strongest—attacked Sahil Sir. I didn't think, I just... acted. My eyes saw through them, deeper than ever before. And then, suddenly, their souls—" Ishan clenched his fists. "I trapped them. Their bodies fell, but their souls were caught in some kind of void, a dimension only I could access. I could feel them struggling, but I had full control. I could absorb, destroy, or imprison

them forever."

Silence filled the room.

Ravi finally exhaled. "Infinity Eyes..." His voice was filled with both pride and concern. "You are a true Rathore."

Ishan looked up. "What do you mean?"

"This ability—it was once wielded by Lord Vijay Rathore, one of our clan's greatest warriors. But only a few in history have been able to awaken it. You are one of them." Ishan's heart pounded. Lord Vijay Rathore... my ancestor?

He grinned. "If this power is so strong, then I can use it to defeat Dev!"

Ravi's expression darkened. "Do not be reckless, Ishan. This power is both a gift and a curse. Overusing it will destroy your eyes. If that happens, not even I can save you."

Ishan's excitement faltered. "Then... how do I control it?" "Through training. You must strengthen your body and mind before you can wield such a technique properly."

Ishan nodded, determination flaring in his eyes. He reached into his pocket and pulled out a small scroll—his Warrior Form. He handed it to Ravi.

"For you, Grandfather."

Ravi took it, a hint of pride in his eyes. "You are growing fast, Ishan. But the path ahead is still long."

The Assembly Hall and Its Security

The Assembly Hall of the Anti-Asura Community was a colossal stone structure, its walls lined with ancient carvings depicting battles from ages past. Towering pillars of black marble reached high into the domed ceiling, supporting intricate chandeliers that glowed with a soft golden light. The floor was polished obsidian, reflecting the flickering torches that lined the perimeter.

At the center of the hall was a massive round table made of dark oak, its surface engraved with the assign of the
   Seven Elder Guardians. Each seat was a throne-like chair, carved uniquely to represent the power and status of the Guardian who sat upon it.

Outside the hall, over a hundred elite warriors stood on high alert, clad in black armor, their faces hidden behind masks that bore the emblem of the Anti-Asura faction. Twenty high-ranking ninjas were positioned inside, their presence a silent but firm reminder that security was paramount. The atmosphere was tense, knowing that an attack was always a possibility.

The Arrival of the Guardians

One by one, the Seven Elder Guardians arrived, each accompanied by a squad of personal guards. Their footsteps echoed through the hall, mixing with the low murmur of warriors stationed around the perimeter.

1. Ravi, the Sixth Elder Guardian, entered first, his deep blue robe swaying as he took his seat. His eyes carried the weight of wisdom, but his aura still radiated the power of a warrior who had fought countless battles.

1. The First Elder Guardian, a towering man with silver hair, was the next to arrive. He wore golden armor, representing his authority over the council. His gaze was sharp,

surveying the hall as if preparing for war.

1. The other five Guardians followed, each representing a different strength—strategy, defense, knowledge, combat, and leadership.

As they settled into their seats, a hushed silence fell over the hall.

The Debate on the Exam's Location

The First Guardian leaned forward. "We are gathered today to decide the center for the Warrior Exam. It must be a location that ensures fairness and absolute security."

A Guardian in a crimson cloak spoke first. "The Himalayas would be the ideal place. The altitude and harsh conditions would test our warriors' resilience, and it would be difficult for any Asura to invade such terrain."

A murmur of agreement swept the table, but the Third Guardian raised his hand. "No. We must hold it in our village. We already have an arena, a highly trained security force, and magical barriers. We can't afford to send our strongest warriors away while the Asuras lurk in the shadows."

The debate grew heated, voices clashing like swords in battle. Some argued that the Himalayas provided natural protection, while others insisted that staying within the village ensured tight security and better organization.

Ravi finally spoke, his voice calm yet commanding. "We must consider the risk. If an Asura invasion happens, are we prepared to defend both locations at once?"

Silence.

The First Guardian nodded. "Then we will hold the exam in the village. Our army will fortify every entrance, triple security patrols, and activate all magical defenses."

The Security Measures

A head warrior in dark armor stepped forward, unrolling a large map of the village.

"Our border patrols will increase to 200 warriors. The outer gate will have two layers of magical barriers, designed to instantly incinerate any Asura who tries to enter. Five hundred elite guards will be stationed at key points, with additional snipers positioned on rooftops.”

A Guardian narrowed his eyes. “And what about internal threats? If an Asura disguises itself as one of us?”

The head warrior smirked. “We will conduct daily scans using detection spells. Any impostor will be exposed.”

The Guardians exchanged approving glances. The village would be a fortress.

A Spy Arrives with a Vital Report

Just as the meeting was concluding, the doors burst open.
    A figure, cloaked in shadows, knelt before the table.

"A report from our spies," he said, handing a sealed scroll to the First Guardian.

The Guardian unrolled it, scanning the contents with narrowed eyes. "This is a list of the ninja participants from around the world—their skills, weaknesses, and ranking."

He placed the scroll on the table for the others to see.

Some were masters of Mantras, wielding spells so powerful they could change the course of battle.

Others specialized in sword fighting, capable of cutting through steel with a single strike.

Some were magic users, controlling elements or summoning spirits to fight for them.

Ravi's expression darkened. "This information is critical. We must prepare accordingly."

Sahil Sir's Training Orders

The First Guardian turned to a warrior standing at the edge of the hall. "Summon Sahil Sir."

Moments later, Sahil entered, his injuries from the last battle still visible, but his determination unwavering.

"You will personally train our warriors," the Guardian ordered. "Ensure they are ready to face the strongest participants."

Sahil saluted. "I will make sure that not a single ninja loses in this exam."

The Fifth Guardian leaned forward. "This is not just about the Warrior Exam.

It's about our reputation. If we fail, we lose the trust of the world."

The Fourth Guardian turned to the head warrior. "Double the security. We cannot give the Asuras even the slightest chance."

The hall fell silent.

The decision had been made.

Conclusion

As the Guardians left the assembly hall, the warriors outside stood at attention, their eyes burning with determination.

The village would soon become the center of the greatest warrior competition in history.

And the battle against the Asuras had only just begun.

Chapter 7: The Path to Mastery

Pushing Beyond Limits

The morning sun bathed the Anti-Asura Academy in golden light as Ishan stood in the middle of the vast training field, sweat dripping from his brow. His fight against the stone guardians in the forgotten temple had revealed new truths about his power, but he knew knowledge alone wasn't enough. If he wanted to stand a chance in the Warrior Exam, he needed to sharpen his skills—physically, mentally, and magically.

His grandfather, Ravi Rathore, watched from the edge of the field, arms crossed. "You've improved," he admitted.

"But you still lack endurance. If you fight like this in the Warrior Exam, you'll be finished in minutes."

Ishan wiped the sweat from his forehead. "Then push me harder."

Ravi smirked. "Good. Because this is going to be the hardest training you've ever faced."

The First Stage: Strength and Endurance

Ravi led Ishan to the mountain path behind the academy, where steep stone steps stretched endlessly into the sky. At the top stood a heavy iron bell—the training goal.

"Your task is simple," Ravi said. "Climb these steps one hundred times—with these."

He tossed Ishan a pair of iron weights, each weighing 50 kg. Ishan's arms nearly buckled as he caught them.

"Are you serious?" he gasped.

Ravi raised an eyebrow. "You want to defeat Dev? Then stop whining and start climbing."

Ishan gritted his teeth and began his ascent. Each step burned his legs and back, but he refused to stop. His Infinity Eyes helped him focus on his breathing, allowing him to distribute his energy efficiently.

By the 50th lap, his muscles screamed in protest, but Ravi stood at the bottom, arms crossed, watching.

"You're slowing down!" Ravi called.

Ishan clenched his jaw and pushed forward.

By the 90th lap, his vision blurred, and his legs wobbled, but he forced himself up. On the 100th lap, he reached the top and rang the iron bell, sending a deep echo through the

valley.

Ravi smiled. "Now, you're ready for real training."

The Second Stage: Weapon Mastery

The next challenge took place in the Academy's underground training hall, where weapons from every era of the Rathore Clan were stored.

"Pick one," Ravi instructed.

Ishan hesitated. He had trained with swords and kunai before, but here, every weapon held a story. He reached for a twin-bladed spear, feeling a strange connection to it.

"Interesting choice," Ravi said. "That belonged to Lord
   Vijay Rathore himself."
   Ishan spun the spear in his hands, feeling its weight and balance.

"Your goal is to defeat me," Ravi said, drawing his own katana. "And I won't hold back."

Before Ishan could react, Ravi vanished and reappeared behind him, swinging his blade. Ishan barely blocked it with his spear, the impact shaking his arms.

"Faster!" Ravi shouted, launching a series of rapid strikes.

Ishan dodged, using his spear to parry. He tapped into his Infinity Eyes, predicting Ravi's movements—but Ravi was faster than any enemy he had faced.

A sudden shock wave from Ravi's blade sent Ishan flying backward. He crashed into the wall, gasping.

"Lesson one," Ravi said. "Speed matters more than strength. Again!"

They fought for hours, Ishan improving with each clash. By the end, his hands were bloody, but his reflexes had sharpened.

Ravi nodded in approval. "You're learning. But you're still not ready."

The Final Stage: Awakening Hidden Power

On the third day, Ravi led Ishan to a sacred waterfall deep in the mountains.

"This place was used by Rathore warriors for centuries,"
    Ravi said. "It will awaken your true potential."

Ishan stepped beneath the thundering water, the impact hitting him like a thousand punches.

"You must control your inner energy," Ravi said. "Focus.
    Find the core of your power."

Ishan closed his eyes, feeling the power of the Infinity Eyes stir inside him. He began channeling his soul energy, trying to manifest it outside his body.

Suddenly, the air around him shimmered, and a dark blue aura erupted around him. The water split around his body, as if obeying his energy.

His Infinity Eyes burned brightly, and for a brief moment, he saw visions of the past—of Dev, of Lord Vijay Rathore, of a war yet to come.

Ravi stepped forward, smiling. "You've unlocked it. Now... you're ready for the Warrior Exam."

Chapter 8: The Art of Combat

Dawn of the Final Training Phase

The sun barely peeked over the horizon when Ishan arrived at the Academy's grand training grounds. His body still ached from the intense training with his grandfather, Ravi Rathore, but there was no time for rest. The Warrior Exam was approaching fast, and he needed to refine every skill— his physical abilities, his Infinity Eyes, and most importantly, his combat techniques.

Sahil Sir, now fully recovered, stood in the center of the field with his arms crossed. Around him, other warrior candidates trained—some wielding swords, others controlling elemental energies, and a few practicing ancient mantras that could summon divine forces.

"You've built your strength," Sahil Sir said as Ishan approached. "Now, it's time to turn that strength into something lethal."

Ishan nodded. "I'm ready."

"Good," Sahil Sir smirked. "Because today, you fight."

First Lesson: The Martial Arena

A group of senior warriors formed a circle around an open air combat pit. The ground was worn from countless
   battles, and the air buzzed with anticipation.

"Here, we fight without magic," Sahil Sir explained. "Only raw skill, strength, and speed matter."

Ishan stepped forward, rolling his shoulders. His first opponent was a muscular warrior named Veer, an expert in hand-to-hand combat.

"First one to land five clean hits wins," Sahil Sir declared.

Veer wasted no time, lunging at Ishan with a devastating punch. Ishan barely dodged, countering with a quick elbow strike to Veer's ribs.

One point.

Veer grinned. "Not bad, but can you keep up?"

He unleashed a flurry of lightning-fast punches, his fists blurring in the air. Ishan blocked some, but one hit his side—hard.

One point for Veer.

Ignoring the pain, Ishan shifted his stance. He remembered Ravi's lesson: Speed matters more than strength. He ducked low, sweeping Veer's legs out from under him. As Veer stumbled, Ishan landed a quick strike to his chest.

Two points.

Veer roared and rushed forward, but Ishan saw an opening. Using his training, he grabbed Veer's wrist, twisted, and flipped him over his shoulder. Veer crashed onto his back.

Three points.

The crowd of warriors cheered. The match continued, but Ishan overpowered Veer with precision. By the end, Ishan stood victorious with five points to three.

Sahil Sir nodded. "Good. You've learned control. But this was only the beginning."

Second Lesson: Weapon Combat

After a short break, Ishan entered the weapon training chamber, a vast underground hall filled with an arsenal of legendary weapons.

Sahil Sir stood before him, holding two wooden swords.

"Today, we train with weapons. Pick one."

Ishan studied the weapons—swords, spears, axes, and daggers. He felt drawn to a pair of twin swords,

lightweight but deadly.

Sahil Sir tossed him a practice version. "Your goal is to disarm me."

Ishan charged forward, swinging with speed, but Sahil Sir effortlessly dodged.

"Predict your opponent," Sahil Sir instructed. "Think two steps ahead."

Ishan slowed down, focusing his Infinity Eyes. Suddenly, he could see the slightest movements in Sahil Sir's stance— a shift in balance, the tightening of his grip, the flicker of his eyes.

Anticipating Sahil Sir's next move, Ishan spun low, his swords striking at Sahil's wrist. The wooden blade flew from his hand.

A moment of silence.

Then Sahil Sir grinned. "That's what I wanted to see."

Third Lesson: Energy Manipulation

Sahil Sir led Ishan to a sacred training hall, where warriors practiced channeling their inner energy into powerful
 attacks

.

"Now, we focus on your magic," Sahil Sir said. "Show me your Infinity Eyes."

Ishan took a deep breath, activating his Infinity Eyes. A dark blue aura surrounded him as his eyes glowed
 intensely. The air shifted, and Sahil Sir took a step back.

"Impressive," Sahil Sir said. "But can you control it?"

Sahil Sir summoned a spiritual orb, a floating mass of energy. "Trap this."

Ishan focused, reaching out with his mind. The orb trembled, then suddenly vanished into the void of his Infinity Eyes.

Sahil Sir's eyes widened. "You did it... You can manipulate souls."

Ishan exhaled. The power inside him felt unstable,
   unpredictable, limitless.

Sahil Sir placed a hand on his shoulder. "With this ability, you will be feared. But be careful—this power will consume you if you overuse it."

Ishan nodded. "I understand."

The Final Test: Survival Combat

Sahil Sir guided Ishan to the Forest of Trials, where warriors were left to survive for 24 hours against various Asura-like training creatures.

"You're on your own," Sahil Sir said. "No one will help you.
    You must rely on everything you've learned."

The test began. Creatures of shadow emerged from the trees—some with bladed limbs, others with piercing red eyes.
    Ishan dodged, his twin swords flashing. He cut through the beasts with precision, channeling his energy into his
    strikes.

Hours passed. The creatures grew stronger, faster, more aggressive. Ishan's body ached, but he refused to give in.

At dawn, he emerged from the forest, exhausted but
    victorious.

Sahil Sir clapped. "Congratulations. You've completed your training."
    Ishan stood tall. He had faced his limits and surpassed them.

He was ready for the Warrior Exam.

Chapter 9: The Gathering of Warriors

T he village was no longer the quiet, disciplined place Ishan had known. It had transformed into a battlefield before the war—a gathering place for warriors of unmatched skill, each preparing for the most grueling test of their lives.

Massive banners bearing the insignia of the Anti-Asura
Community hung from stone pillars at the village gates. Elite guards in black armor patrolled the perimeters, each equipped with enchanted weapons capable of detecting and neutralizing any Asura infiltration. Watchtowers had been reinforced, and archers stood poised, their eyes scanning the horizon for any sign of movement.

The streets buzzed with activity. Warriors of various ethnicity and backgrounds, their uniforms and emblems denoting their homelands, filled the marketplace, speaking in different tongues, exchanging techniques, and testing each other's strength in friendly duels. Blacksmiths were overworked, forging last-minute weapons, while merchants sold potions, scrolls, and talismans rumored to enhance combat abilities.

Ishan walked through the crowded streets, his mind focused. This was his first real step toward proving himself—not only as a warrior but as a true Rathore. He clenched his fists, his Infinity Eyes glowing faintly as he observed the fighters around him. He could sense the tension, the hidden blood lust in some, and the pure determination in others.

At the heart of the village stood the Grand Arena, an enormous structure made of reinforced stone, enchanted to withstand even the most destructive techniques. It had been built specifically for the Warrior Exam, and today, it would witness the first of many battles. Inside, thousands of warriors gathered, waiting for their names to be called.

The Elder Guardians Convene

Within the heavily guarded Assembly Hall, the Seven Elder Guardians stood around a grand table, each carrying the weight of leadership and war on their shoulders.

First Guardian, Surya Dev – A towering man with golden armor, representing the strategic mind of the Anti-Asura forces.

Second Guardian, Vedika Rai – A woman whose mastery of illusion magic made her one of the deadliest warriors in history.

Third Guardian, Yashwant Sen – A seasoned warrior who had survived countless battles against the Asuras.

Fourth Guardian, Bhairav Singh – Known for his brute strength, he was a one-man army.

Fifth Guardian, Rameshwar Nath – A scholar of war, responsible for designing the village's security.

Sixth Guardian, Ravi Rathore – Ishan's grandfather, carrying the wisdom of his ancestors.

Seventh Guardian, Kaushal Thakur – The enforcer,
   ensuring discipline among warriors.

The hall was surrounded by fifty elite warriors, armed and ready. The windows were protected with powerful barrier seals, ensuring that no enemy—human or Asura—could eavesdrop.

A scroll was placed on the table. It contained the names of every warrior participating in the exam, sorted by skill set:

Mantra Users – Specialists in ancient chants and elemental magic.

Sword Masters – Fighters trained in legendary swordplay.
   Stealth Assassins – Masters of silent killings and poisons.

Physical Combatants – Warriors who relied purely on their bodies.

A spy entered the room, handing over another scroll. "This contains information about potential infiltrators. We suspect some Asura spies have disguised themselves as participants."

Ravi opened the scroll and scanned the names. His expression darkened. "We must be cautious. If even one of these infiltrators makes it through, this exam could turn into a massacre."

Surya Dev nodded. "Security has been strengthened. The entire village is surrounded by a protective barrier, maintained by our top magicians. Even if an army of
   Asuras arrives, they won't breach it easily."

Vedika Rai smirked. "But we must also be prepared for deception. Asuras are clever. They will find a way to disrupt the exam."

Ravi sighed. "That's why we must train our warriors harder than ever. We cannot afford to fail."

The Final Preparations

As the sun began to set, a massive drumbeat echoed through the village, signaling the start of the Warrior Exam Registration.

A large crowd gathered at the registration booths, where exam officials handed out numbered tags to each participant. Ishan stepped forward and received his number: 273.

Sahil Sir, now fully recovered, approached him. "This is it, Ishan. The moment you've been training for."

Ishan nodded. "I'm ready."

From the rooftops, unseen eyes watched. Among them was Dev's left-hand man, observing the preparations with a smirk. He whispered into a magical scroll, sending a message to his master:

"The village is fortified, but they are unaware of our plan. We strike soon."

133

The battle had not yet begun, but war was already in motion.

Chapter 10: The Parkour Trial, and the Arrival of Chaos

The day of the first Warrior Exam trial had arrived. The village was in an electrifying state, filled with warriors and ninjas from all over the world. The morning sun cast golden light over the grand arena, its massive stone walls stretching high, adorned with ancient runes of protection. Hundreds of elite guards patrolled the area, their eyes scanning every movement.

The village was fortified like never before. Magical barriers shimmered around the perimeter, and archers stood on rooftops, ready to strike at any intruder. The Elder Guardians had ensured that not a single Asura could step inside unnoticed.

The crowd gathered in the massive examination square as the officials called the names of the participants.

— Exam Proctor –

"Attention, warriors! Your numbers have been assigned. These numbers will determine your match ups and battle order. May the strongest prevail!"

Ishan glanced at the scroll he received—his number was
273. Around him, warriors from different countries adjusted their weapons, some whispering mantras, others flexing their fingers, preparing their magic.

— Ishan (thinking) –
"So many powerful warriors... I can feel their energy. This is going to be intense."

The first trial was a Parkour challenge, designed to test agility, reflexes, and endurance. The goal was to reach the end platform of the giant obstacle course—a colossal wooden and stone structure filled with swinging axes, collapsing bridges, spiked walls, rotating pillars, and narrow ledges suspended over deep chasms.

A massive gong echoed through the sky, signaling the start.

— Exam Proctor –
  "BEGIN!"

Hundreds of warriors dashed forward.

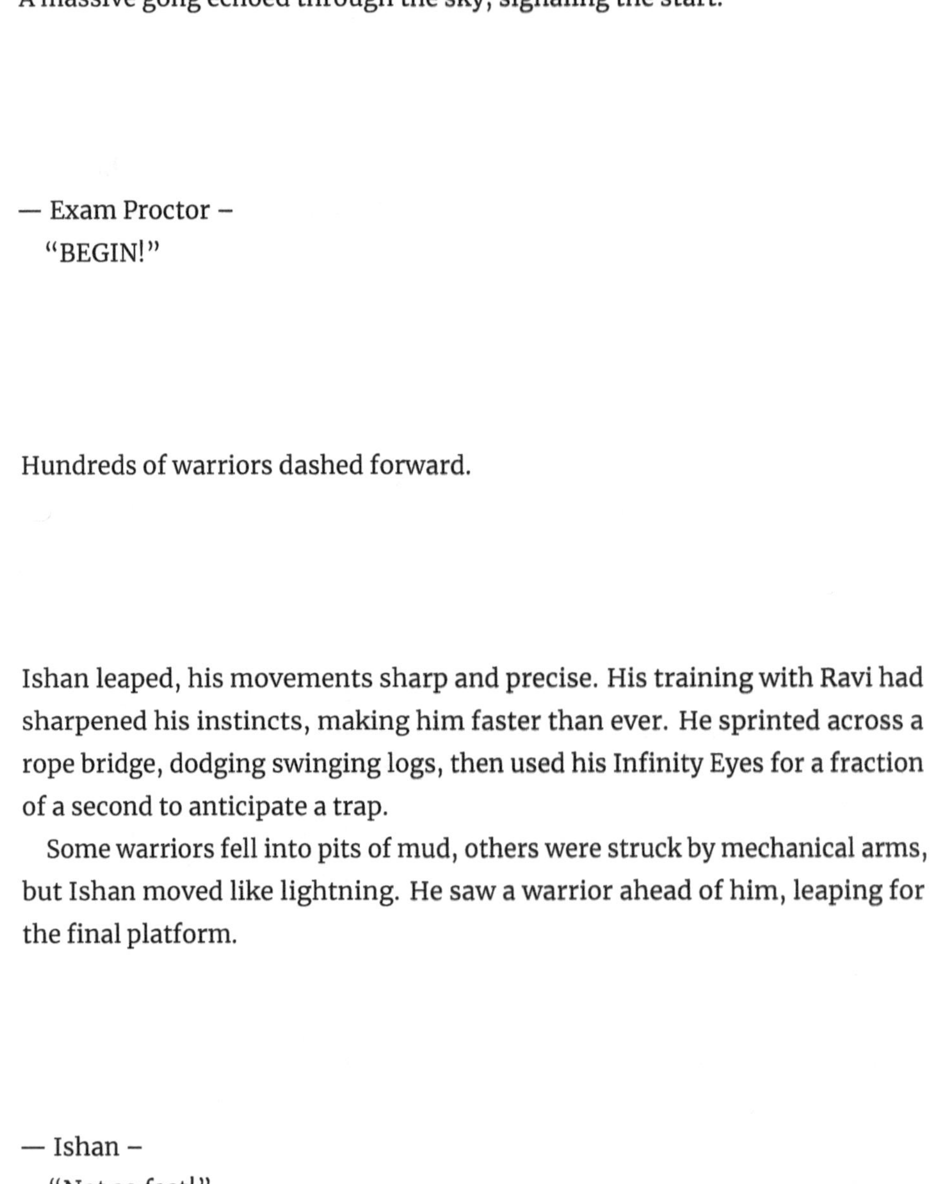

Ishan leaped, his movements sharp and precise. His training with Ravi had sharpened his instincts, making him faster than ever. He sprinted across a rope bridge, dodging swinging logs, then used his Infinity Eyes for a fraction of a second to anticipate a trap.

Some warriors fell into pits of mud, others were struck by mechanical arms, but Ishan moved like lightning. He saw a warrior ahead of him, leaping for the final platform.

— Ishan –
  "Not so fast!"

He kicked off a wall, flipping mid-air, grabbing onto a hanging chain, and swinging past the warrior to land in the top 20 finishers. The crowd erupted in cheers.

Meanwhile, in the Shadows...

Far beyond the village, Dev stood inside a dark temple, surrounded by his generals. He unrolled an ancient scroll, inscribed with blood-red symbols.

— Dev –

"It is time. The village believes it is safe. Let's show them the true meaning of war."

With a single chant, the scroll ignited, and a massive pulse of dark energy shot into the sky.

Back in the Village – Battle Round Begins

The next stage of the exam had begun—the one-on-one battles.

— Exam Proctor –
"Match 4: Ishan Rathore vs. Ajay Chakravedi!"

Ajay was a tall, muscular warrior from a distant land, dressed in red robes, carrying a massive broadsword.

The battle began, and Ajay charged with immense speed. Ishan barely dodged as the ground split apart from Ajay's strike. Their clashes were fierce, but then—

— ?? –
"Enough of this nonsense!"

A dark figure leaped into the battlefield—Dev's left-hand man. He unrolled a scroll, and before anyone could react, a wave of magic spread across the arena.

The ground cracked, and a terrifying transformation began. The entire battlefield started morphing into something unnatural.

The air darkened, trees burst out of the ground, vines crept over buildings, and the village was swallowed into an endless jungle biome.

Millions of Asuras emerged, their red eyes glowing, their
   snarls filling the air.

Ishan and Ajay stood back to back, their battle forgotten.

— Ishan –
   "What... what is this?!"

— Ajay –
   "We're surrounded... this is a battlefield now."

The village alarms blared, and the Elder Guardians rushed to action. But the chapter ends as the chaos unfolds, leaving the fate of the exam—and the village—hanging in the balance.

TO BE CONTINUED...

About the Author

Hello everyone! My name is Ikshit Gautami, and I am 15 years old from Jhansi, Uttar Pradesh. Worthy for a God is my first book, and it represents all my hard work and dedication.

I first wrote this story when I was 13 years old. A friend recommended that I watch anime, and at first, I thought it was just cartoons. But after watching Naruto, Solo Leveling, Demon Slayer, and My Hero Academia, I realized that anime is more than just animation—it's an emotion. That's when I decided to create my own anime.

At first, I spent all my time thinking about my anime, even in funny moments like in the bathroom! I wanted to animate it, but my digital drawing skills weren't good enough. I felt like my dream would remain just a thought. However, one day, I decided to turn my anime idea into a novel.

At 15, I realized that I was lazy at handwriting but fast at typing, so I finally sat down and wrote my story.

This is just Volume 1 of Worthy for a God, and I hope you enjoy the story! I have taken inspiration from many great anime like Solo Leveling, Naruto, Demon Slayer, and My Hero Academia. This novel contains intense action and violence, and I hope you love the adventure!

Thank you for supporting my journey as a young author!

You can connect with me on:

🌐   https://www.instagram.com/the_younger.novelists?utm_source=qr&
igsh=MWY0aG5pMjdqZGZxNA==

www.ingramcontent.com/pod-product-compliance
Lightning Source LLC
Chambersburg PA
CBHW031143130726
47988CB00006B/2501